CRIME
CLUB

CRIME CLUB

Melodie Campbell

orca soundings

ORCA BOOK PUBLISHERS

Library and Archives Canada Cataloguing in Publication

Title: Crime club / Melodie Campbell.
Names: Campbell, Melodie, 1955– author.
Series: Orca soundings.

Description: Series statement: Orca soundings

Identifiers: Canadiana (print) 20190065850 |
CANADIANA (EBOOK) 20190065869 | ISBN 9781459822382 (softcover) |
ISBN 9781459822238 (PDF) | ISBN 9781459822405 (EPUB)

Classification: LCC PS8605.A54745 C75 2019 | DDC jc813/.6—dc23

Library of Congress Control Number: 2019934052
Simultaneously published in Canada and the United States in 2019

Summary: In this high-interest novel for teen readers, sixteen-year-old Penny is surprised when her dog digs up a skeleton in the backyard.

*Orca Book Publishers is committed to reducing the consumption
of nonrenewable resources in the making of our books. We make
every effort to use materials that support a sustainable future.*

Orca Book Publishers gratefully acknowledges the support for its
publishing programs provided by the following agencies: the Government of
Canada, the Canada Council for the Arts and the Province of British Columbia
through the BC Arts Council and the Book Publishing Tax Credit.

Edited by Tanya Trafford
Cover images by Shutterstock.com/Annette Shaff (front) and
Shutterstock.com/Krasovski Dmitri (back)

ORCA BOOK PUBLISHERS
orcabook.com

Printed and bound in Canada.

22 21 20 19 • 4 3 2 1

For Dave

Chapter One

"We're moving *where*?" I heard Mom pronounce the name but thought I must have heard it wrong.

"Mudville. South of Toronto, on Lake Erie. We're moving in with your aunt Stella," said Mom.

I relaxed a bit. I know Aunt Stella from family reunions in Cape Cod. She is my mother's older sister. I like her a lot.

And I'd heard of Toronto, of course. It is a big city. Not big by New York standards, maybe. But we weren't actually going to live in Toronto.

"Mudville. Seriously?" I asked. "So what's in Mudville? Besides mud?"

Mom paused. "Not a whole lot. Apparently they're known for their pickles. And they have a big fish."

Fish? "Just one?"

"It's a statue. There's also a fishing regatta. The Mudcat Festival, I think it's called."

"Why on earth would they ever move to Canada?" I said. "It's winter all year round! More important, why are *we* moving there? You know I'm allergic to snow."

"Uncle Phil inherited a pub. Since he died, your aunt has been all alone. She runs the pub now. We're going to live above it. And it is *not* winter all year round. Mudville is just north of the border."

"We're going to live in a pub? Now *that's* cool," I said.

"I thought you'd like that part," said Mom, rolling her eyes.

A change of scenery would probably be good. Things had been tough the last few months. High school sucked. And I don't mean the homework. People avoid you when they know your dad is in prison. They ghost you. It changes everything, and it's not fair.

None of this was my fault. Or my mom's.

"But this is only until I finish high school, right?" I said. "We'll be coming back here eventually."

Mom raised an eyebrow. "Let's take it one step at a time. It will be nice to get a fresh start."

I heard the words she didn't say. *Without your dad. Without the shame and fear that follow us everywhere.*

"We'll get you there next week. Then I'll wrap up things here and be in Mudville by the end of the month. Is that okay with you?"

"We're taking Ollie, right?" I felt the first signs of panic. Going anywhere without my dog was out of the question, as far as I was concerned.

"Of course! He's part of the family."

Ollie is a huge dog of unknown pedigree. A better name for him would have been Scruffy.

"What's the pub called?" I asked.

"The Big Dill," said Mom. "Because of the pickle factory."

Hard to believe, but true. One week later, I saw it all for myself.

Chapter Two

I have a secret. Not even Mom knows this one.

I'm still talking to my dad. We found a way.

After Dad was charged, Mom and I were hounded by journalists. They parked in front of our house, with vans and cameras. They followed me to school. You can imagine the headlines they were after. *Interview with the Killer's Daughter*. It was awful. If this is what rock stars go through, I never want to be one.

I dropped out of school in June to avoid them. Mom had to leave work. It was like we were prisoners ourselves. So when she said we were moving to Canada, I couldn't wait. But here's the thing.

Dad's lawyer was worried about people tracing our correspondence and figuring out where we lived. The tabloids were annoying, but this was more about the Mob. The lawyer said we couldn't have any contact with Dad at all. That was the only way we could drop off the radar. Be safe.

So Dad and I don't send emails. But we do write them.

I'm particularly proud of the system we've been using, because I thought of it myself. I created a new email account.

I gave Dad the password before he was hauled off to jail. Every few days, I go in and leave a message in the Drafts file. Dad logs in from his end and reads the draft message. Then he deletes it and writes his own.

No emails sent. Nothing to trace.

This is what he wrote last night:

Hi, Bugs. Thanks for letting me know where you're going. All okay here. It's tough inside, but I'm used to tough. Don't worry about me. Let me know how you settle in. Love you.

When I was little, I couldn't say my own name, Penny. It came out Bunny. So Dad started calling me Bugs, as in Bugs Bunny.

It made me feel good when he called me that in the email. It also made me sad. I miss him so much.

Dad accepted a plea in order to get a lighter sentence. That's what the lawyer told us. But I know better. He pleaded guilty to avoid a trial. In a trial, everything comes out.

I don't know why he killed that man. No one would tell me. They said it was safer for me not to know.

But one day I'll find out.

Everything went according to plan. Mom drove me to the border. Aunt Stella was waiting there, ready to drive me and my stuff (and Ollie) to Mudville. She even got me a new cell phone. One with a Canadian phone number.

Mom would join us a week later. We wouldn't communicate again before then, just to be safe. I hugged her tightly as we said our goodbyes.

It was a beautiful summer day. Aunt Stella and I arrived in Mudville just after lunch. She parked the car around back. As we walked up the sidewalk, Ollie bounding around us like a maniac,

Aunt Stella gave me a side hug. "Welcome to the Big Dill. Everyone around here calls it the Dilly. It will be great having you here. I've been pretty lonely since Phil died."

I hugged her back. Maybe this would be a good thing for her too.

Aunt Stella looks a lot like Mom, only older and a bit slimmer. Her shoulder-length brown hair was pulled back with clips. Her great big smile was irresistible.

The door to the pub looked freshly painted. The top half was all screen. The bottom half had a picture of a smiling green pickle wearing sunglasses. Not kidding. The door swung inward easily.

Ollie beat me in the door. I stepped across the threshold. It wasn't as dark inside as I had expected it to be. My eyes easily adjusted. Lots of light poured in from windows on three sides. A man with gray hair sat at a round wooden table by one of the windows. He looked up and squinted.

"Jeez Louise, Stella. They've finally gone and done it. Crossed a poodle with a grizzly bear."

Aunt Stella darted ahead of me. "Now you behave yourself, Vern."

"Or is it a woolly mammoth?" said Vern.

Aunt Stella gave Vern a playful swat. "Thanks for looking after the place this morning. This is my niece, Penny. And this gorgeous boy is Ollie." She reached down to scratch Ollie behind the ear. She didn't have to reach down very far, of course. "Never mind the grumpy old man, Ollie. Good boy. Aren't you a handsome fellow."

Ollie started to whimper. He wanted more scratches. Some guard dog he was.

Vern stood up. He was much taller than I had expected. Close on six feet.

He shuffled up to us and peered at me with surprisingly blue eyes.

He put out a large, knobby hand. "I'm Vern."

Ollie growled.

"Ollie, stand down," I commanded. "Friend." Ollie relaxed. He wagged his bushy tail and yipped. "Nice to meet you."

"Wait until you meet Wolfgang," Aunt Stella said, still rubbing the pooch.

"Who's Wolfgang?" I asked.

"Tara's dog. You'll meet them both soon. In fact…" Aunt Stella turned to look at the back door. "That will be Simon now," she said. "He and his friends wanted to be here to welcome you."

"That's nice," I said. Simon is my cousin. From Uncle Phil's first marriage. Aunt Stella and Uncle Phil used to bring him down to Cape Cod most summers. I like Simon, although he is sort of nerdy. He likes old movies and things.

Simon is a year older than me. I am counting on him to help me adjust to the new school in the fall.

I looked up at the sound of a motorcycle. I heard it roar, then *putt*, *putt*, then come to a stop somewhere close by. I peered out the back window and stared in amazement.

"Ah…not Simon. That's Tara. I'll let you two get acquainted. I've got to start prepping for the dinner crowd," said Aunt Stella. "Vern, can you give me a hand back here?"

Vern shuffled obediently after her. Curious. Did my aunt have a boyfriend?

A few seconds later the back door banged open. In marched a tallish girl about my age. And a dog. A sort of dog, going, "Yap, yap, yap. Yip!"

"Damn dog won't wear his helmet," said the girl. "Don't know why I bother."

"Your dog rides in a sidecar?" I asked. *Wow*.

"His name is Wolfgang. I'm Tara." She gave me a crooked grin.

Wolfgang was a pug of enormous plumpness and smallish voice.

Ollie came bounding down the stairs. I grabbed for his collar and held on tight. But I might have saved my strength.

Wolfgang started to do laps around Ollie. "Yap, yap, yap, yap!" The yapping didn't stop. Neither did the circles.

Ollie stared at the thing leaping around him. I let go of his collar and held my breath. He just sat. Wolfgang stopped doing laps and padded cautiously up to Ollie's front.

Ollie leaned forward and licked him.

"Aw. He likes you." Tara reached down to scratch Ollie.

I breathed a sigh of relief. It was important to me that people here wouldn't have a problem with Ollie.

"Hi, Tara!" Stella called from the kitchen. "Is Simon with you?"

"Any minute," said Tara, looking up. "They were right behind me."

I went back to the window just in time to see a black Mustang pull up. Holy crap—a Mustang! Two people got out, both male, both tall. I watched them amble up the walkway.

The taller guy reached for the door and opened it. As he did, the two dogs ran out of the house.

"It's okay," said Simon. "We closed the gate." He came over, and we shared an awkward hug. "Hey, Penny. Nice to see you. Cool that you're moving here."

"Thanks." I returned his grin and pushed back. He was rail thin and tall. I figured he was even taller and thinner than the last time I'd seen him. We both have dark hair. Mine is quite a bit longer than his though.

"Here they are," said Simon. "This dude is Brent. You've already met Tara.

They're twins. Not identical, of course. Although they do look alike." I had noticed they both had the same shaggy blond hair. "Brent's my best bud."

Brent grinned and lunged for Simon.

"Hey!" Simon ducked away. "Don't touch the hair!"

I covered a snicker. Simon was more vain than I'd expected.

"You look a lot like that television star," Tara said to me. "Doesn't she, Brent?"

"Which star?" I asked.

"You're right. She does," said Brent to Tara. Then he answered me. "The one on *New Girl*. With the big gray eyes."

I liked the sound of that.

Vern came out from the kitchen.

"Hi, Mr. Evans," said Simon. "You know Tara and Brent."

"'Course I do. You can all call me Vern. If you're old enough to drive, you're old enough to drop the *mister*."

"Vern, get back in here," my aunt called. "I need you to reach something."

Vern shrugged his shoulders and smiled. "The lady calls."

A few minutes later we had pulled up chairs around a table.

"Give me your cell," Tara said to me. "I'll text each of us from your phone, so we have your number too."

"Cool," I said. I happily handed over my new cell.

"Love your car," I said to Brent.

He grinned. "Over three hundred horsepower. It's a beast."

"That car is his baby," said Tara, handing me back my phone. "He's up all night with it sometimes."

"Tara found it for me. She works in a garage after school," said Brent. "Comes in handy." He smiled at me.

I couldn't help but smile back. Tara and Brent had the same light-green eyes.

"Brent and I work at the local grocery store," said Simon. "Maybe we can get you a job there too."

"I think Aunt Stella expects me to work here at the pub," I said. "Not serving drinks. I'm not old enough. But helping with the food and stuff."

Simon smacked his hand to his head. "Of course. I'm a dope."

"I'm sixteen now. I want to get my license soon," I said.

"Brent could teach you how to drive," said Tara. "He taught Simon."

I would not mind that a bit. Not only did Brent have a hot car, but he was also pretty hot himself.

The scratching at the back door got louder. I went to open it. Wolfgang trotted in, proudly carrying a big bone.

"Would you look at that?" said Brent. "That's quite a prize."

"Where did you get that old bone, fella?" said Tara. "Is there a compost heap out back or something?" she asked us.

"Nope," Simon said. "What's Ollie doing out there?"

I was still holding the door, so I took a look. Ollie was at the far corner of the herb garden, digging like he was tunneling to China. Dirt was flying in every direction.

"Hey," I yelled to him. "Ollie! Stop that!" *Oh no!* Ollie had already dug up a bunch of plants and showed no signs of stopping. His head was already well down into the dirt. I ran out to grab him.

"Boy, can he dig," said Brent, right behind me. The others followed too.

"Bad dog!" I scolded as I reached for Ollie's collar. "How could you *do* this?" Aunt Stella was going to have a fit. What a terrible thing to happen on our very first day here.

I stopped dead.

Ollie was a complete mess. His face was covered in muck. But his eyes gleamed. He was clearly very proud of his unburied treasure.

We all stood there looking at the skeleton Ollie had just uncovered. A human skeleton.

"Whoa," said Simon. "Guess we know where Wolfgang got that bone."

Chapter Three

"Holy crap," I said finally. I was having a heck of a time keeping Ollie controlled. I couldn't let him get too close to the edge of the hole he had dug. But even from here I could see that a corpse had been placed or rolled face first into the shallow grave.

"That guy didn't die naturally," said Simon. He pointed to the skull, which looked crushed at the back.

I felt a little sick.

"How old are these bones, do you think? They have to be pretty old, right? I mean, they're just bones." I spoke quickly.

Brent poked around the dirt with his shoe. "Looks old, all right. What do you think, Tara?"

"Yup. Probably over twenty years."

Now it was my turn to stare at Tara. "How do you...?"

She shrugged. "It's just bones. The rest is gone. They look white. Soil is pretty acid around here."

I shivered. How did she know this stuff?

"Tara's a brainer," said Brent.

"I'm going to med school when I finish high school. Dead things don't gross me out," said Tara.

"Looks like a man," said Brent. "Big shoulders. See?"

"Definitely a man," said Tara. "A tall one."

How had she figured that out? I tried to follow her eyes, but the whole skeleton wasn't uncovered.

"Long torso," she said, reading my mind. Things were going to get uncomfortable pretty quick if she kept reading my mind. Like they weren't uncomfortable already. Dead body. First day.

"This is where the firewood used to be piled," said Simon. "Aunt Stella didn't want to deal with that anymore. So she got a gas fireplace installed a few months ago. We just moved the wood last week."

"So that's why the skeleton hasn't been dug up before," I said. That and the fact that the backyard was fenced in. Big predators would have to jump a six-foot fence. Did they even have big predators in Mudville?

"How long was the woodpile there?" asked Tara.

"For as long as Uncle Phil owned the place. Before we were born," said Simon. "Stella would know exactly."

"So the body has probably been here for twenty years," I said.

"Who do you think it is?" said Tara.

"No idea," said Brent.

Ollie woofed. He nearly pulled my arm out of its socket, trying to get back to his treasure.

"I'm just going to put Ollie inside with Wolfgang," I said. I walked to the back door, dragging the bouncy mutt all the way. It was a battle to get him on the other side of the door, but eventually I won. "You stay there," I ordered him, closing the door firmly. Luckily, the door opened inward. All his pawing against it wouldn't force it open.

I turned around. Nobody had moved. I could see them talking urgently among themselves. They stopped as I drew close. We all stared down into the makeshift grave.

"What should we do?" said Simon.

"What do you think, Tara?" Brent said. I found it interesting how he deferred to her.

"We should probably send for Simon's uncle Bob." Tara looked at her twin.

"He's a cop," Simon explained to me. "Other side of the family."

I froze. The last thing I needed was police asking a bunch of questions. It wouldn't take them long to figure out who Mom and I were related to. Word would get around. I didn't want to be known as the kid whose father was in prison.

I was so lost in my thoughts, I almost missed the odd silence that had fallen over the others.

"Or," Simon continued after the long pause, "we could simply cover it up again. Let the poor guy rest in peace."

He glanced over at me. Thing is, Simon knows. He knows Mom and I wouldn't want any police hanging around the place, looking for murderers. He knows I would vote with the "bury the evidence" club.

But even so—even though I was up against a wall—I couldn't help wondering. Was Simon suggesting this option to protect our identities? Or was there some other reason he didn't want the body investigated?

"We could still investigate," said Tara. "Just quietly, among ourselves." It was hard not to notice the longing in her voice.

"And if we found out anything interesting, we could present it to the police," said Brent. I felt his eyes on me.

Okay, now I was suspicious. Simon must have told Tara and Brent why I had moved here. I grabbed Simon's arm and pulled him away from the others.

"You told them." I kept my voice low so no one else would hear.

Simon's face went red.

"It was supposed to be a secret, Simon!" I felt betrayed.

"I only told them your dad was in jail. And that you were here to lie low. Nothing more."

I turned my head so I could see Tara and Brent. They were looking down into the hole. Talk about awkward.

"We need their help," Simon pleaded. "Don't be mad."

I wasn't mad so much as embarrassed. But I had more important things to worry about. Keeping the cops away was number one. I gave Simon a look, and we joined the others.

"Shall we take a vote?" Tara said. "So far, only the four of us know about this."

"And Ollie," said Simon. "And Wolfgang."

"And the dogs," said Tara with a small smile. "We'll have to do something to keep Ollie from digging up this spot again, if we…" Her voice trailed off.

"So…who is in favor of keeping the status quo?" said Brent.

"Let sleeping dogs lie?" said Simon.

Tara gave him a stern look. "Hands up for reburial."

Four hands shot up.

"All in favor. Good," said Tara. "It's always awkward when someone disagrees."

Like this situation wasn't awkward enough.

"You realize that we're probably breaking all sorts of laws," I said.

"Don't get lost in the details," said Tara. "Harry is the important one here. Do you think he wants his bones laid out on a hard, cold steel slab in the police morgue? To be examined like a lab rat?

I wouldn't. We're doing what's best for Harry."

"Harry?" I almost shouted it.

"Not his real name, of course," said Tara. "But we need to give him a name. It's only decent. And Harry is more fitting than John Doe."

More fitting than…was Tara nuts?

Simon snorted. "I get it. *The Trouble with Harry*. That old Hitchcock movie. Harry gets buried and dug up and reburied and re-dug up all through the film."

"That's it." Tara nodded. "You made us watch it last fall. So we're agreed that we will cover up poor Harry while we investigate. But we need to do a better job of it this time. And somehow cordon off the area so the dogs can't get at it."

I swung my gaze around the yard, looking for something that we could use. Nothing.

"Okay, we don't have much time," said Tara. "Simon, can you find a shovel so we can fill in this hole?"

Simon nodded. "For now we can just fill in the hole. Brent and I can do the plants tomorrow."

I glanced toward the pub. "I should probably check on the dogs. And keep Aunt Stella from getting suspicious."

"We'll take care of things the best we can back here," said Simon. "Catch up with you later."

I nodded. As I walked away, I heard Tara say in a low voice. "Do you think it could be Earl?"

Chapter Four

I found my aunt in the kitchen. Vern was nowhere to be seen.

"Hey, Aunt Stella, who is Earl?" I asked.

Stella stopped rolling pastry. She glanced up at me and then down at her work again. "How on earth…?"

I didn't know how much to tell. So I kept it simple. "Something Tara said."

Stella went back to rolling. "Earl Offerson was an older distant cousin of the twins. He ran off with another woman about twenty years ago."

So that's what the others were thinking! That maybe this Earl guy didn't leave town with the other woman. Maybe he'd stuck around to warm the ground.

And if so, did his wife kill him? Or did the other woman? Or her husband?

"It was a bit of a scandal," said Aunt Stella. "We didn't live here then. We used to have our own house before Phil died. We rented out the upstairs of the pub to a woman named Sally Hooke."

I got it now. Why it was awkward for her. They owned the love nest but hadn't known it was being used for that purpose. "Is that who Earl ran off with? Your lodger?"

Aunt Stella put down the rolling pin. She looked me right in the eye. "What brought this up, Penny?"

I hesitated. My hands curled around the back of the wooden chair I was standing behind.

"Come clean," she said. "If you're going to live here, you're going to have to trust me. And vice versa."

She was right. I didn't want to have any secrets from Aunt Stella. So I told her about Wolfgang's bone. And then about Harry.

"Well, darn," she said. "So Simon and Brent are out there refilling the hole?"

I nodded.

Aunt Stella was silent for several moments. I watched her forehead furl into long lines. Finally she picked up a tea towel and started wiping flour off her hands.

"Not a good idea, having the cops around. Especially on your first day here. Your dad…well, we don't want anyone to know about that, now do we?"

She took a deep breath. "So they're willing to keep it a secret, right?"

I nodded. I knew she was referring to my new friends.

"Those kids are smart. We'll keep it between ourselves. Although, if you don't mind, I might tell Vern. No one else though."

Relief! It felt good to have an ally. I am really lousy at keeping secrets from people I love. I sat down with a plunk in the wooden chair.

"You'll meet Jean Offerson tonight. Earl's widow. Both she and Dotty Dot are coming here. They're inseparable."

I tried to work it out. But no, it wasn't happening. "Dotty Dot?"

"Dorothy Danvers," said Stella. "Dot for short. She's slipping, if you know what I mean. Rather ditzy. So we call her Dotty Dot."

I had no idea how to respond to that.

"Funny thing about Earl," said my aunt. "I haven't thought about him in years. We all just assumed…"

I could see she was reading my mind. That maybe he hadn't run away. Maybe he hadn't gotten farther than the backyard of the Big Dill.

I checked on Ollie. He and Wolfgang were napping. I decided not to disturb them. A few minutes later I went back outside. Simon had found a spade and a snow shovel. He and Brent had the hole almost filled. Tara was supervising.

I swallowed hard. "Okay, slight change of plans," I said. All three looked over at me.

Tara said it first. "You told Stella."

I shuffled my feet and nodded. "She figured something was up. I couldn't lie to her." I could see Simon was not happy to hear this. "But it's okay!"

I added. "She agrees that we should all keep quiet about it. After all, it was a very long time ago." *Besides, you told Tara and Brent about me*, I wanted to say to him. But I didn't.

"The murderer is probably dead by now," said Tara.

Brent was standing with both arms leaning on the snow shovel. He had a big frown on his cute face. "Have you thought about why your aunt might want to keep this quiet?"

Yes. I had thought about it, actually. It was her property. Could she and Uncle Phil have had something to do with it? I told them what I had just learned.

"They owned the place. But they didn't live here at the time," I said. I told them, too, about the lodger, Sally Hooke, running off with a man called Earl.

I saw Tara dart a look at Brent. He was looking at her too. Then he nodded.

I wasn't surprised. After all, Tara had been the first one to mention Earl. They just didn't know I had overheard.

"So. What do we do now?" said Simon.

"Finish covering up the grave," said Tara. "And don't tell anyone else." She gave me a stern look.

"I won't," I said. "Don't forget—I have the most to lose."

"But we should get investigating," said Tara. "You know what we could do first?"

"What?" I asked.

"Track down Sally Hooke. If Earl is still with her, then we'll know the bones aren't his."

"Even if they aren't together, Sally might know what happened to him," I said. But she also might know that it *is* him in the ground, I thought. A warning flashed in my brain. But before I could think it through, Simon said something that distracted me.

"Brent, can you do a trace?" *A what?* Simon turned to me. "Brent's a whiz with computers," he said.

Brent? Not Simon? I stared at Brent. "You don't *look* like a nerd," I said.

Brent raised one eyebrow. "Oh? What does a nerd look like exactly?"

I could feel my face going red. *What a stupid thing to say!* Just because someone was hot didn't mean they couldn't be smart. I was an idiot.

"Tara, we need to get home. But I'll bring my laptop tonight," he said. "See you at seven."

"Tonight?" I said. "Why? What's happening tonight?"

Simon grinned at me. "It's your first night in Mudville. The whole town will be coming to the pub."

Simon wasn't kidding. People started to arrive right at five. A few came via the back door. Simon's uncle Bob, the cop, came in the front. He gave my aunt a quick hug and then sat down with Vern. He was a big guy, with a shaved head and a great smile. Seemed friendly rather than scary. I took his order and started back to the kitchen. That's when the commotion started.

A shout came from outside the pub, and then I heard several more raised voices. I hurried toward the back door, but Bob was quicker. He reached the door first and swung it open.

Ollie trotted over. He had a huge bone in his mouth.

The dogs had dug up another bone.

Chapter Five

"Shit, shit, shit," said Vern. He hung on to the doorframe, panting. "Who let the dog out?"

I stifled a hysterical giggle. By this time Aunt Stella had joined Vern in the doorway.

"It's probably just an old soup bone," said Aunt Stella. Her voice was unusually high.

"That doesn't look like a soup bone," said Bob. He gave my aunt a pointed look. Then he walked swiftly to the gravesite.

It was as bad as I could imagine. When customers had come in the back way, Ollie must have squeezed out. And he had dug up the bones again. A small circle of people stood gaping into the hole.

"Shit," said Vern again.

We watched Bob pull a cell phone from his pocket. No question that he was calling the station. I felt my forehead break out in a sweat. Had we left any trace? Would Bob figure out that we had already seen the skeleton?

At that point, I made a decision. I followed Bob out to the scene of the crime. He didn't know I had seen it before. I had to make it seem like this was the first time.

I gasped loudly, looking down at the human bones.

Bob turned. "Get back in the pub," he said, waving a hand. He turned to the other gawkers. "You people, go home. Penny, tell everyone in the pub to go home. I'll talk to you later."

Vern and Stella had crept up behind me. We hurried back into the pub. Vern gave everyone there the bad news. We had the place to ourselves within minutes.

"I'm sorry," said Aunt Stella. "I should have thought about Ollie getting out."

"We should lock the front door. Put the Closed sign up," Vern said.

"Good idea," said Aunt Stella. "Penny?"

I rushed to the front door, locked it and switched the sign around. As I came back, Bob was dragging Ollie by his collar back into the pub. Minus the bone.

"Don't let this dog out again. Don't let anyone else come out." He directed this to me. I met his stormy eyes and nodded. The door banged shut behind him.

"At least he doesn't think you and the kids had anything to do with this," said my aunt. She came over to the kitchen table, carrying a tray with three coffee mugs and a carafe. Her hands were shaking a bit as she set down the tray. Vern moved over to make room for her on the bench.

"Why do you say that?" I said. I plunked down on the bench opposite them.

"You acted totally surprised. I kinda fudged on the soup-bone thing. And Vern kept saying *shit*, like he had something to hide."

"Shit," said Vern.

"So what should we say to the police?" I needed to rehearse it.

"We say nothing," said Aunt Stella firmly. "Ollie just dug up those bones. We don't know who it is or why it is there." She carefully poured coffee into each mug and handed them around. "Penny, you should text Simon and the twins. Let them know what's going on here."

"And tell them to keep quiet," said Vern. "They weren't here. They don't know anything about dug-up bones."

"Except word will get around, Vern," said Aunt Stella. "You know how it is in this town. Everyone will know everything by tomorrow."

"Shit," said Vern.

The pub was shut down. More policemen came. We watched from a window. They put a tent up over Harry's gravesite. Then the crime-scene officers

43

got to work. A young cop in uniform stood guard at the gate.

Aunt Stella made us sandwiches for dinner. Vern left after we'd eaten. I sent text messages to my friends, explaining what was going on. Shortly before eight, I got a text back from Simon.

Can you get out? We're across the street.

I sneaked out with the excuse that I needed to walk the dog. We couldn't let him out to pee in the backyard anymore. Two cops were settling down to interview my aunt. They didn't seem interested in me. I grabbed Ollie's leash from the hook in the kitchen.

Ollie bounded happily out the door, pulling on his leash. He picked up the pace when he saw Simon and Brent across the street at the riverfront park. It took all my strength to keep up with him.

It was a lovely summer night, clear without too much humidity. The sun was getting ready to set.

"Let me take the dog," Simon said. "You guys can talk." I handed over the leash. Simon took off with Ollie, running.

"I did some research online with Simon. We found Sally Hooke," said Brent. "At least, I think it's her. She'd be the right age. I have an address in Hamilton."

"That's terrific!" I said, clapping my hands together. "What do we do now?"

"Simon and I have to work the early shift for the next two days. But Tara is off on Thursday. She said the two of you could go check it out."

"Sure," I said. But I was a little disappointed. It would have been nice if Brent could come too.

"You can report back on Thursday night. We'll be seeing you then, of course." He gave me a lazy smile that did something to my insides.

Ollie was having a grand time too. Simon had let him off leash. It was hard not to smile, watching Ollie bounce along the shore. He picked up a big stick and came trotting over with it, proudly dropping it at my feet. Then he went charging back to get another.

Simon jogged back to us, puffing a bit. "Did you tell Penny the plan?"

"Everything except your travesty on Thursday night," Brent said.

Simon punched him on the shoulder. "Hey! It's a class act. Even Tara thinks so."

"What's happening Thursday night?" I said.

They both grinned at me. "You'll see," said Brent.

After they walked me back to the Dilly, I set to unpacking my suitcase.

The bedroom my aunt had given me was painted a cheery peach color. The bed was a four-poster, already made up. Two windows looked out on the street below. I put my suitcase on the old wooden chair between the windows. A white set of drawers was only steps away. I quickly transferred my stuff to the drawers.

Right before I went to bed, I checked my Drafts folder. No word from Dad yet. This wasn't unusual. Sometimes he was a few days in responding.

I left him another message. I told him about the new friends I had made. I didn't tell him about the body. He had enough to worry about.

Here's the thing. You don't get to choose your family. My dad has always been good to me. I know he loves me. He may have done something terrible. But he is still my dad, and I love him.

Life shouldn't be this complicated.

Chapter Six

It was kind of weird waking up to silence. I was used to the constant noise of traffic in the city. And yelling. People yell all the time in New York, at every hour of the day and night. This place was eerie. How could it be so quiet with the windows wide open?

Two texts were waiting for me.

From Tara: **All set for Thursday. Pick you up at ten.**

From Brent: **Do you like fishing? I have Sunday off.**

I answered both immediately. **Sure** and **Sure**.

Brent wanted me to go fishing with him! How cool was that?

I threw on a T-shirt and jeans and shuffled down the wooden stairs in my slippers.

I got to the bottom and looked around. "Ollie?"

Somewhere not far away, I could hear the thumping of a tail on the planked floor.

Morning light streamed in through the east windows. Dust motes floated in the air. I followed the sound of thumps to the kitchen.

Vern was already there, drinking coffee. Definitely a boyfriend, I thought.

Ollie was at Vern's feet, munching on scraps. We said good morning, and I headed to the cupboard for a coffee mug.

"Worms," I said out loud. "Where do you get them?" Vern would know.

My aunt looked up, startled. "Oh, Penny. I'm so sorry. You get them from dogs. But they've got drugs for that, and they work quickly. Honest." She looked down at the dog. "Ollie, you naughty boy. We'll have to get you some medicine too."

"What?" I said, confused. "No! I mean I need to get some worms."

Both of them looked at me like I had dropped in from outer space.

Vern started to wheeze. "Must be some weird American thing, Stella."

Granted, I didn't know much about fishing. "So you *don't* use worms for fishing here?"

Vern chuckled. "Oh! Well, in my opinion, chubs are better for mudfish."

"Oh, now I get it," said Aunt Stella, laughing. "Are the boys taking you fishing, Penny?"

"Brent is. On Sunday," I said. I could feel my face turning red.

"Oh. Well, that's a few days off," said my aunt. Her eyes twinkled. "You're seeing Brent already?"

"We're trying to see if we can track down Sally Hooke," I said, desperate to change the subject. *Crap!* I hadn't intended to tell them about the investigation.

"Oh, Penny. Do you think that's wise?" asked my aunt.

"Why not? I think it's a good idea," said Vern. "Don't you want to know who did the deed?"

"Well, it was a long time ago. The murderer is probably dead by now," said Aunt Stella.

"What murderer?" said a breathy voice.

Two women stood at the entrance to the kitchen. I hadn't heard them enter the pub. Ollie was happily circling them, like a herding dog.

"We're talking about a TV show, Dotty. Hello, Jean. Have you met Penny yet?"

A tall hawklike woman stood over me. "Would know you anywhere. You look so much like your aunt. Dotty, doesn't she look like Stella did when she was younger?"

Dotty lived up to her name, starting with her shoes. Which didn't match. Her full skirt was a wild paisley print. Topped with one of those unfortunate peasant blouses.

"Oh," she said in that breathy way. "You're Penny. Penny." She looked puzzled. "Like a—what is it, Jean?"

"A coin. A penny," said Jean.

Unfortunately, there didn't seem to be a lot going on behind Dotty's pretty brown eyes.

I put out my hand. "Pleased to meet you."

Jean's grip was strong and firm. Dotty smiled and put her hands behind her back, like a shy child.

Jean turned to Aunt Stella. "What's this I hear about a body?"

I nearly dropped through the floor.

"Gosh darn, Jean. How'd you hear about that already?" said Vern.

Jean shrugged her narrow shoulders. "Bob's mom. I came over as soon as I heard."

"Well, please keep it to yourself," said Aunt Stella. Her stern face reminded me of a teacher I had in fifth grade. "It had been buried for a long time."

"At least twenty years," said Vern. "Shove over, Penny. Make room for these two."

I'm not sure exactly how it happened. I do remember that Dotty was looking down at the table, not paying much attention to the conversation. Then she suddenly gasped. Her glazed eyes became alive and focused.

"Jean, the body. Do you think—?"

Jean clapped a hand over Dotty's mouth. "Stop that. We're not talking about it." She waited a moment, then dropped her hand.

"But could it be—?"

"No, Dotty," said Jean firmly. "Don't say anything."

Dotty stared at her.

"It's a secret," said Jean.

I watched Dotty grapple with that word. "A secret," she said.

The others nodded and looked relieved. I was still nervous.

Chapter Seven

Jean and Dotty left to go shopping. Aunt Stella didn't waste any time.

"Hand me your phone," she said. "I'm going to call Trudy."

Who's Trudy?

Vern seemed to hear me and leaped to interpret. "Dr. Fowler's old receptionist," Vern explained. "There was only one dentist in town back in those days. We all went to him. Dr. Jennings took over the practice about twenty years ago. Trudy still works there part time."

Aunt Stella was determinedly punching numbers on the keypad. We all waited.

Her face changed to friendly. "Trudy, hi. It's Stella. I'll get to the point quickly, because time is of the essence. Do you still keep old dental records? I mean, of people who died, say, thirty years ago?"

Vern and I leaned forward.

"Yeah... Yeah. Makes sense... Hmmm..." Aunt Stella sat back. "Okay, just a heads-up, hon. Bob will probably be in to ask the same question. Don't tell him I called, okay?" She looked up and winked at us. "Love to you and the grandkids."

She clicked off and faced us. "About ten years ago they put all their files on computer. But only the active files, of course. All the dead people were taken out and destroyed."

Vern snorted.

"All the dead people's *files*, I meant." She glared at Vern. "Jeez. A person can't say anything around here without some clown twisting it around."

"I didn't say anything," Vern protested.

I didn't allow myself to get distracted by their banter. "So that means they won't be able to tell who the...um... dead person is from their teeth," I said. I didn't know whether to be relieved or not.

"Not unless they lived in town and died less than ten years ago. Which leaves out our skeleton," said Aunt Stella. "Bob is going to be pissed."

"Now wait," said Vern. "They might be able to extract DNA from teeth. I'm pretty sure they can."

"Oh, right," said Aunt Stella. She seemed to sink a bit in her seat. I watched her closely. It was pretty clear she didn't want this victim identified. What was she afraid of? I couldn't believe she'd had anything to do with the murder. I just couldn't.

Vern left shortly after lunch. I wasn't sure it was his idea. I took Ollie for a quick pee out front. When I returned, Aunt Stella was carrying her purse.

"Penny, I want you to come with me," she said.

"Where are we going? Can we take the dog?"

"No dog. Jean has a cat."

So we were going to Jean's house. I followed her to the front door.

Ollie didn't mind being left behind. He settled down for another nap.

Outside, a stiff breeze was blowing off the river. It made the hot sun bearable.

"I've thought about this for a while now," said Aunt Stella. "We need to warn her. It's the decent thing to do. But I didn't want to use a phone, where someone could overhear."

I had figured as much. But Jean? Aunt Stella suspected Jean had something to do with this?

"Thing is, Jean is vulnerable. Oh, she doesn't seem like it, with her gruff exterior. That's just an act. She likes to play the older sister around Dotty Dot. Helps them both feel more secure."

To our right, the old row housing gave way to detached homes. Aunt Stella turned at the second one and marched up the walkway. I followed obediently, noting the well-kept garden. I always notice flowers. My Italian grandmother had a flower store in New York.

Aunt Stella knocked. Jean opened the door. When she saw Aunt Stella, she smiled.

"Jean, we need to talk to you."

Maybe it was the tone of my aunt's voice, but the smile faded. Jean stepped back to let us in.

The house was Victorian, with a small parlor up front. Jean led us into the parlor and motioned for us to sit down.

Bookshelves lined every wall, leaving only the front bay window and fireplace free. The dark stain of the wood carried through to the floor. No rug. Lots of brown. It was all far too gloomy for me.

I looked around for a cat. Guess they didn't like company.

As Jean waited for us to begin, she regarded us with a stern expression. I noticed her hands were clenched in a tight ball.

"Now prepare yourself, dear. This isn't pleasant." Aunt Stella leaned forward. "You know about our little bones-in-the-backyard problem."

I started to interrupt. She stopped me with her palm up. "No, let me finish, Penny. Thing is, I heard Bob say something about dental records."

"Holy cow," said Jean.

She sat very still. I could see she was thinking hard. "So you think—?"

"No, I don't," Aunt Stella interrupted. "But it doesn't matter what I think. I've checked with Trudy. They don't have dental records that go back that far for people who aren't still patients."

"Dental records," said Jean. She looked down at her hands. "You're thinking it could be Earl."

"No. I don't think it's Earl. The police have a few possibilities, people who disappeared around that time. We can expect them to follow up on all of them. They have to."

"But *they* think it could be Earl," Jean said and then stood up abruptly. "Time for tea."

She marched out of the room without looking back.

Aunt Stella leaned back with relief. "That went well."

I stared at her. "Are we speaking the same language?"

"What do you mean?"

"This new definition of the word *well*," I said.

Aunt Stella had the grace to smile. "No hysterics. No frantic denials. Jean knows now, so we've done our duty. She can deal with the police when they come. I should tell her to find some old clothes of Earl's, in case they want to do a DNA test."

"Would she still have them? I mean, it's been over twenty years."

"People here don't throw out good things," said Aunt Stella. She waved a hand. "This isn't the city. You live in those small condos, of course you have no room for old things. Our basements are stuffed with things that might be useful to someone someday."

Jean wasn't long with the tea tray. She set it down on the worn brown coffee table.

"Stella, one lump for you?" she asked.

"Two," said Aunt Stella. "You know what I always say. Tea without sugar is vegetable soup." She winked at me.

"How do you like your tea, Penny?" Jean asked.

"Left in the pot," I said.

That got a small smile out of her. "Why didn't you say so?"

"I drank a gallon of coffee right before we came. All I need is the bathroom."

Jean turned and pointed to the stairs. "Up and to the right."

I found the bathroom no problem. I also found the cat curled up on the bathmat. It lifted its marmalade head and surveyed me briefly. Apparently I was not a threat.

When I returned to the parlor, Jean was just coming up from the basement. She had a red-plaid hunting jacket in her hands. It looked ancient.

"This was Earl's," she said to Aunt Stella. "No one's worn it since." She shook it to release the dust. It fell from the garment like fake snow in a snow globe, swirling through the air.

Aunt Stella put down her tea cup. "Perfect. Don't try to clean it in any way. Just have it handy."

"I'll put it in the back closet," said Jean. She disappeared again.

"We should probably leave now," Aunt Stella said to me. "I don't want to be here when the cops come. Let's go out the back way."

Jean reappeared. We said quick goodbyes and left by the kitchen door. The old sidewalk we followed back to the pub was broken up at random intervals. I had to focus to make sure I didn't trip.

Aunt Stella was quiet. I wondered what she was thinking about. I know what I was thinking. If the body in the backyard wasn't Earl, then who *was* it?

Chapter Eight

"Never underestimate the power of a village grapevine," said my aunt, hanging up the phone. "That was Bob's mom, saying the police have just been to Jean's."

I had to smile. Aunt Stella had been one step ahead of them.

It was late afternoon now. I'd been thinking about motive.

I locked my hands around the warm mug of coffee. "Aunt Stella, I know you said you don't think it's Earl's skeleton we found. But you still wanted to warn Jean anyway. So why would you think Jean might have killed Earl?" I asked.

Aunt Stella sat back. She frowned. "I don't know. To get him out of her life?" she replied after a moment.

"But that's just it. He *was* getting out of her life. He was running off with Sally. So why kill him? What would she gain from it?"

"Good point," said Aunt Stella. "They didn't have much money, those two. So it couldn't have been for financial reasons." She paused. "Earl was a loser. I don't think he ever worked a real job in his whole life."

"Wow," I said. I knew all about men who didn't have real jobs. "So how did they pay their bills?"

"*She* worked. Had a job in her father's drugstore."

That wouldn't bring in much money. "Did Earl look after the kids?"

My aunt snorted. "Not a chance. Not back then. Jean's mother looked after the kids. Earl always had these 'schemes' going. Oh, he was a dreamer, that one." Aunt Stella took another mouthful of coffee. "Always had some crazy business idea. He'd talk people into lending him money to get things started. Then he'd lose it all, of course. Eventually he ran out of people to hit up. And that's when he turned nasty."

I took a sip from my mug and nodded. I wanted to encourage her to keep talking. This was all so interesting.

"Earl started drinking. Beat Jean up a few times too, although she hid it well. But *we* knew, Dotty and me. Women who wear long sleeves all the time? It's to cover up. They grab you here."

She pointed to her upper arm. "It leaves bruises."

I knew about that too. One of my great-aunts...

I leaned forward. "But that's what I mean. Jean would have been happy to see him go, wouldn't she?"

Aunt Stella fiddled with her coffee mug. "True. If it had been me, I would have been jumping up and down with glee. Hell, I would have packed his bags, filled the car with gas and handed him the keys."

Silence filled the room.

"So you *don't* think it's Earl's body?" Aunt Stella finally asked.

"I don't know. Jean doesn't seem to have a strong motive. But it still could be him, I guess. Someone else could have killed him," I said. "Someone he borrowed money from?"

"Maybe we should talk to Vern about it. He'll be here soon."

I raised an eyebrow. "Fine with me. But what are you thinking?"

Aunt Stella sighed. "Well, now you've got me thinking about who else it could be. Earl isn't the only man who has gone missing from Mudville in the past forty years."

I had been waiting for this. "Who else did you have in mind?" I asked.

"It's tricky," she said. "But I seem to recall a young man disappearing when I was a teenager. A draft dodger from the Vietnam War. Do you know about the Canada connection?"

I shook my head. I knew about the Vietnam War, of course. We'd learned about it in school.

"Canada probably wasn't very popular with the American government back then. We decided to open our doors to draft dodgers. It was pretty easy to cross the border in those days. You could do it with a driver's license."

She paused to sip her drink. "I used to feel sorry for those boys. They weren't much older than you."

Suddenly having to leave your country and all of your friends and family? That was something I could totally relate to.

"You think someone may have killed a draft dodger?" I said.

"It's a possibility," said Aunt Stella.

The back door of the Dilly opened, then clanked shut. I could see Vern making his way toward us. Ollie leaped up to greet him.

Coming in from the bright sunshine must have temporarily blinded Vern. He paused, squinting. Then his face brightened when he saw us at the kitchen table. Or, rather, when he saw Aunt Stella.

"Shove over, Stell," he said as greeting.

"Hello to you too," said Aunt Stella, shaking her head. But she shifted over on the bench to make room for him. "Hey, do you remember when that draft dodger went missing?" she asked him.

"Eh?"

"It would have been in the 1970s."

The lines on Vern's face deepened. "Yeah. Young skinny guy with the long hair and big mustache? Used to do odd jobs, I remember."

"That's the one. I was still in school then. But I remember people talking about how he disappeared one day."

"We all thought he just left for Toronto. You're thinking the body in the backyard could be him?" Vern said.

"Possibly. But I have no idea why someone would kill him."

"Was he hanging around any of the highschool girls?" I asked. "A draft dodger wouldn't be very popular with the fathers in this town." No steady job. And a deserter, according to some.

"That's a fair point," Vern said.

"Aunt Stella?" I prodded.

She seemed deep in thought. "I was thinking about what Penny said. Maybe the draft dodger got a young girl pregnant. It happened a lot."

"Surely the pill was available," I said.

"Yes, it had been around for at least a decade, but you still had to visit a doctor to get it. And a lot of doctors wouldn't prescribe the pill to unmarried women, let alone to young girls. They certainly wouldn't do it without telling their parents."

"That's harsh," I said.

Aunt Stella shrugged. "It was a different time. A time none of us would want to go back to."

Vern grunted. "What do you have to do to get a drink around here?"

"Have a coffee, Vern. I just made a pot," said Aunt Stella.

"You're no fun, woman," muttered Vern.

I smothered a giggle. Some couples are married before they're married.

Vern left after dinner. I went upstairs to check my Drafts folder. Nothing from Dad yet. I texted Tara to confirm our trip the next day. Tonight I'd spend some quiet time with Ollie.

The cops still had the backyard cordoned off. That meant we couldn't open the pub for business yet. This was fine with Aunt Stella. Tonight was book club, and she often had to miss it.

"You should join us, Penny," she told me. "Meet some more neighbors."

"You just finished saying they were nasty," I said.

"Only when they have to read CanLit," she said.

Chapter Nine

The next morning I packed Ollie's small travel bag. Two bottles of water, bowl, puppy snacks and bandanna. I stuck a few of my own things in there as well, so I wouldn't have to take a purse. Then I went downstairs, where I found Stella already at the coffeemaker. Coffee, fresh bread, bacon...my nose was in heaven.

"Tara here yet?" I asked. I slung the bag on a chair.

Stella handed me a mug. "Not yet. You would have heard her." She reached down to scratch Ollie. "He's already been out for pee and had his breakfast."

"Thanks, Aunt Stella. You're spoiling this ol' guy here." I watched as she offered him another slice of bacon.

Ollie stopped begging. He stood still with his head cocked to one side. With a leap, he took off to the back door. Sure enough, within seconds I heard the unmistakable *vroom* of Tara's bike. Then the characteristic *putt-putt* as she shut it off.

I quickly finished off my breakfast and slurped back my coffee. Then I grabbed my jacket from the hook and the travel bag.

"Bye!" I called out to my aunt. The door clicked shut behind me.

Tara was heading down the walkway already. The dogs danced around each other.

"Wolfgang's in fine form today," she said. "Ate a sock for breakfast. I expect it will show up in an hour or two."

I scanned the parking lot for a car. No car.

"So how do we do this?" I said. "Take a bus?" Did they even have buses from here to Hamilton? Now that I thought about it, I hadn't seen any buses in Mudville.

"Of course not," said Tara. "We'll take the bike."

The bike? I looked over at Tara's motorcycle as we exited the yard. It was pretty old. I'd never ridden in a sidecar before. The dogs would be disappointed, of course.

"I'll put the dogs back in the Dilly," I said.

"No need," said Tara. "They can ride in the sidecar."

"With me?" I squeaked.

"Don't be silly, Penny. There wouldn't be room. The dogs get the sidecar. You can ride on the back with me."

Two dogs, two people—one bike. This would be an adventure you didn't get every day in New York.

I took Ollie's bandanna out of the travel bag and fastened it around his neck.

"Wolfgang, I think you better let Ollie in first." Tara reached down to pick up her dog. "Penny, you get Ollie in there. I'll hold the little guy."

I stared at my huge dog, and I stared at the sidecar. How did one get Ollie-size canines into sidecars?

We tried a few ways. First, I got into the sidecar to show him how it was done. He got in, too, before I could get out.

Which meant I had to push him off me before I could get out, and then we were both on the outside again. This was a great game. Ollie loved it.

"Can you lift him in?" said Tara.

Lifting wasn't a good option. A hundred pounds of wriggling, squirming mutt is not easy for one human back to handle.

So I tried option two. Outsmart the critter.

Simple, really. I needed to convince him this was another game. So I pretended I was about to get into the sidebar. He leaped in before me, therefore winning the game.

Both of us were happy. Tara deposited the pug between Ollie's front legs, and all was cool. I tucked Ollie's bag in behind him.

"Wolfgang won't be able to wear his helmet," said Tara. "It might hurt Ollie if we stopped suddenly. But I have one for you." Tara unstrapped a second helmet from the back.

Tara put hers on. I did the same. She climbed aboard, and I slipped on behind her. I put my arms around her waist and looked anxiously over at the dogs beside me. No need for worry. Ollie wasn't trying to get out. If Wolfgang was happy to stay put, Ollie would do the same.

A few minutes later, we were whipping along River Road, heading north. Mudville was an hour from Hamilton if there was no traffic. We would likely get there in half that time. Tara's bike apparently had only one gear—warp speed.

This seemed to suit the dogs just fine. Me? I was practically giving Tara the Heimlich maneuver just to stay on the back. I was also pretty sure I'd swallowed a bug.

A 4x4 pickup came at us from the other lane and honked. Tara raised her right arm in a jaunty salute, and the bike sashayed wildly.

"Hands on the bike!" I hollered. My words got lost in the wind.

We turned from River Road onto a country lane. With no traffic to worry about, I felt my heartbeat return to normal. The rural scenery was quite pretty. We passed a horse racetrack and some mighty rich-looking stable properties.

That's when it happened. We saw a police car pulled over on the side of the road. Too late. We whizzed by it far too fast. *Crap!* Sure enough, a siren split the air almost immediately.

The cop car shot up behind us. Tara slowed down, pulled over to the side and switched off the bike. All of us looked in the direction of the person exiting the black-and-white vehicle behind us.

It was a male officer. About average height. It didn't take him long to cover the distance between his car and Tara's bike.

Holy shit! I recognized him. He was the young cop who had stood guard at the gate the day before when the CSI people were doing their thing with Harry.

Would he recognize me? *Think, Penny!* He hadn't been there when the first officers had arrived. I was pretty sure I hadn't gone outside after Bob had shooed me indoors.

The good-looking cop stared at us. Tara raised her visor.

"Tara Stevens," he said.

"Hey, Randy," said Tara. "I mean, sir."

"You have a dog in your sidecar. At first I thought it was a bear. But now I can see that it's a dog. I think."

Wolfgang decided to commence barking at this point. He didn't like to be overlooked.

"Okay, there are two dogs in your sidecar." The cop scratched his forehead.

"And no bears," I said, trying to lighten the mood.

Tara sat more upright. "We're on our way to Hamilton. Sorry if we were speeding, but the dogs like it. The wind in their faces. I'll slow down."

"I'm pretty sure dogs shouldn't be riding in sidecars," said the cop.

"Why not? Are there laws against it?" Tara asked.

He looked blank.

"I didn't think so," said Tara. "So there also wouldn't be rules about *two* dogs riding in sidecars," she added.

"Besides, Ollie is a therapy dog. See?" I pointed to his bandanna. "He goes with me everywhere."

"And Wolfgang is therapy for the therapy dog," Tara added. "It's stressful work for a pooch."

The cop just stared at us. He shook his head. For a moment I thought he was going to say something, but he just flung both his arms in the air. I'm not sure if he was waving us on or simply flailing at the heavens.

When he walked away, Tara said, "I didn't know Ollie was a therapy dog."

I didn't want to get into it. So all I said was, "Therapy dogs are allowed everywhere. Mom figured it would be a way to keep him by my side at all times. Hence the bandanna."

"No questions asked, with a bandanna," said Tara. "Clever. What does it actually say?"

"*St. Lawdog Therapy Dog.*" I pointed to the cute badge on the fabric.

"You're kidding me."

"Nope. Look it up. It's a real saint. There are four churches named after him in Wales."

"Wales, huh? Now I simply have to go there." She started the bike, and we were on our way again.

Chapter Ten

Half an hour later we were standing on the wooden porch of an old house in the heart of Hamilton. Shabby chic can be a thing in New York. This wasn't that.

Tara pressed the ancient doorbell. Nothing happened. She gave a tentative knock on the door.

"That's not the way you do it," I said, making a fist. I showed her the New York way. We didn't have to wait long.

A young woman with light-brown hair opened the door. She wore blue jeans and a ratty gray tunic sweater. My heart sank. She was much too young to be our Sally.

The woman frowned slightly and said, "We're Catholic."

I stifled a laugh. Of course. Two teenage girls calling on a summer morning—who else could we be? Except we weren't exactly well dressed. And I was pretty sure religious types didn't canvas on motorcycles. Or come with dogs.

Tara jumped in quickly. "Oh, we're not selling religion. We're actually looking for someone we think might live here. Sally Hooke?"

I saw some strong emotion cross the woman's face. Then sadness. "You're a little late," she said. "The memorial service was in April."

Ten minutes later, we were talking like old friends. The woman had invited us in, and now the three of us sat around an old table in the shabby kitchen. The chairs wobbled when you moved. I looked around. Faded white cabinets. Someone had tried hard to get the worn vinyl floor to shine.

Luckily, Sheena Hooke—not Sally— loved dogs. Ollie and Wolfgang, who had been welcomed in even before we were, had set off to explore the inside of the house. Sheena poured coffee into three well-used mugs, then handed ours to us.

"So Sally left you this place. Nice," said Tara. She sipped coffee from a mug that said *Nurses Do It with Care*.

"I was her only niece," said Sheena. "She didn't have any kids of her own, but I guess you'd know that. Who is this guy she was supposed to have run off with?"

"Earl Offerson. They left Mudville about twenty years ago. He's the one we're trying to locate, actually. We were hoping Sally might have an idea where we could find him."

Sheena shook her head. "Sorry. Never heard of him. But I was only a little kid back then. If they ran off together, they must have split up soon after. And if the guy was married, I can understand why the family didn't talk about it." She put down her mug. "Still, it surprises me. Aunt Sally didn't seem the type."

"What do you mean?" I said. I had only been listening up until now.

Sheena shrugged. "I can't imagine Aunt Sally running off with this guy. She never cared much about having a man around. I always figured that's why she was so keen on me being able to support myself."

Interesting. I tucked that one away in my memory for later.

"Aunt Sally helped me through nursing school," Sheena continued. She sipped from her mug. "She invited me to live here while I was going to college, and I just stayed on. Suited us both, you know?"

I nodded. No wonder she had inherited the house.

"I'm sorry she died," said Tara.

"I miss her," Sheena said simply.

"Just a minute. What is that *noise*?" said Tara, looking around.

Gak, sputter, sputter, phhhppptt.

Wolfgang trotted in, gagged, then deposited something on the floor.

We all looked down at a well-slimed something that might have been pink at one time.

"Well, look at that. It was a pair of undies, not a sock," said Tara. "Bad dog."

Tara dropped Ollie and me off at the pub shortly after three. Ollie ran to the kitchen to beg for treats. I gave a wave to Aunt Stella, then dashed upstairs for a shower. Riding a motorcycle is fun, but those helmets are hell on hair. Tara didn't seem to care, but I did. My hair is my best feature. Flat is not a good look for me.

I spent some time blow-drying my hair. Then I got dressed in clean clothes. As I was putting on earrings, my phone pinged. A text from Brent.

Meet me in the pub parking lot now?

My heart did a happy dance. He was here! And he wanted to see me. I rushed to the back door and flung it open.

Brent was standing just beyond the gate. I could see him looking my way.

He wasn't smiling. That should have warned me. But I was so happy to see him, I didn't think. I hurried down the walkway to meet him. He opened the gate before I got to it. In his right hand was Ollie's bag. He handed it over to me.

"You left this in the sidecar," Brent said. "Tara had to go to work, so I said I'd deliver it."

I stared at the bag in my hand. It was hard to breathe. I looked up into his face to see if I was right. He was frowning.

"Normally, I wouldn't open someone else's bag. But I had this stupid idea of putting a surprise in it for you." With his right hand, he pulled a long chocolate bar out of his jacket pocket. "Simon said you like peanut-butter cups. So I stopped at the mini-mart after my shift. It was supposed to be a nice surprise. You'd open the bag sometime later and find them." He paused. "But I was the one who got the surprise."

I gulped.

His eyes never left mine. "Why is there a gun in your bag?" he asked.

I suppose I stood with my mouth open for several seconds. What could I say? If I told him the truth, he might turn away. Never want to see me again. But if I lied, and he later found out…

It wouldn't be any better. It would be worse.

So I gambled. And told him the truth.

"My dad gave it to me. For protection," I said. My heart continued to pound.

His eyes went wide. "Protection? From what?"

I hesitated.

"Does this have something to do with why he's in prison?" Brent asked.

I nodded.

He placed his hand on my arm. "Let's get in the car. We can talk there."

He guided me to the passenger side and opened the door. When I got in, he closed it. Then he went around to his side. The car felt like a cage around me. I wanted to cry. But I didn't.

"You better tell me," he said gruffly.

"It's not that easy," I said. *Nothing is easy anymore.*

"You can trust me," he said. "I can keep a secret. But what the hell, Penny? Tell me why you're sixteen years old and your dad gave you a gun."

"I don't know where to start," I said. I fidgeted on the seat.

"Then start with why you moved here," said Brent, looking directly at me. "What's really going on? Why is your dad in prison?"

I sucked in a breath and said it. "For murder."

I'd never said those words out loud before. My throat felt like I had swallowed ashes.

There was a long pause.

"Shit," said Brent.

Chapter Eleven

"Why?" asked Brent. "Why did he do it? I'm assuming he really did do it?"

"I don't know," I said. It was the truth. I almost relaxed. It was such a relief to stop hiding everything.

"You don't know if he really did it? Or you don't know *why* he did it?"

"Both," I said. "Okay, he pled guilty. I think he probably did it. Mainly because Mom doesn't question it. But I don't know why. No one will tell me." I took a breath. "They say it's for my own protection."

"Shit. That's heavy." Brent leaned his left arm on the wheel. "Sounds for real. Probably it's best you don't know then."

Best, maybe. I knew Dad had connections to the mob. No one ever went into details. If you asked, you got shut down.

"Do you know how to use it?" Brent asked finally.

"Yes. And how to take care of it." I didn't know how much I wanted to tell him. Dad had given it to me on my thirteenth birthday. He'd taught me how to use it. We'd practiced at a family farm near Cape Cod. I was a pretty good shot. He had been proud of me. At the time, I hadn't questioned why he thought I might need to know how to shoot a gun. I just saw it as a cool thing to do.

There were obviously things he hadn't told me. Things that had led to his arrest.

"We'll keep you safe," Brent said firmly.

I turned my head in surprise. His expression made me smile. He looked so determined.

"No, really," he said, gazing fiercely into my eyes. "We're a team, right? You, me, Tara and Simon. Teams protect each other. That's what they do."

"Okay," I said. "But how?"

Wrinkles formed under his blond bangs. "Anytime you're uneasy, call us. One of us will come. You never have to be alone. That's a start."

I thought about that. Not very practical, but I didn't want to break this moment. It was nice having Brent be so concerned about me.

"So can I tell Tara?" he asked.

"Sure," I said.

"But you'll have to do your part and call us," he said.

"I know." I leaned back in the seat. "Don't forget I have Ollie too. That's one of the reasons they gave him to me."

Brent watched me carefully. "For protection?"

I shrugged. "And for company. It's lonely being the only kid of a convicted felon." I knew that sounded harsh. But it was the bitter truth.

"Shit," said Brent again.

We parted soon after that. Brent headed off home with a promise to see me "later tonight." I wondered about that. We were going fishing on Sunday. What was up tonight?

I made my way back inside. Aunt Stella was waiting for me in the kitchen.

"Penny, we've got news. Bob's mother phoned. The DNA isn't Earl's."

Bob should really do something about his mother, I thought. But what

I said was, "That was a quick turn-around."

"Actually, Janet Summerfied's daughter, Lacey, works in the lab now and fast-tracked it when she saw it was from Mudville," said Aunt Stella. "Her hometown."

"Always helps to have a local connection," said Vern, nodding.

Did every small town work this way?

"So the body is someone else's," I said.

"Seems that way," said Vern.

I didn't know what to think about that. It was a setback. With *this* news, clearly we would have to start over.

"Oh, and good news, Penny. The police said we can open tonight," said my aunt. "I'll need your help in the kitchen. It's karaoke night. Everyone will be here. We'll get quite a crowd."

So that's why Brent said he'd see me tonight!

Vern smacked his hand to his head. "Damn near forgot." He groaned. "Tell me it's not country-and-western night, Stella. Don't think I could take country music again."

"What's wrong with country music?" I asked.

"All those lonely men grabbing the mic and wailing hurtin' and cheatin' songs." Vern's face twisted into a grimace.

"What're you talking about?" Aunt Stella winked at me. "Didn't you like 'She Done Me Wrong, so I Did Her In'?"

"Sung by the local butcher, no less," said Vern. "Whiny *and* creepy."

"Hurt his sausage business something awful," said my aunt.

"It wasn't all bad. My favorite was 'You're Roadkill on My Highway of Life,'" said Vern.

"Now that's clever!" I said.

"Thing is, it's good for business," said my aunt. "People drink a lot when they have to listen to bad singing."

"And the more they drink, the badder it gets." Vern chuckled.

"Exactly," said Stella brightly. "But no worries. It's fifties night."

"Well, that's a relief," said Vern. He leaned back on the bench.

"You won't want to miss this," said Aunt Stella. She glanced over to Vern, and they both smiled.

"Why?" Frankly, small-town karaoke was exactly the sort of thing I might plan to miss.

"Just wait," said Vern. "You're in for a surprise." There was a twinkle in his eye. Then he laughed.

Chapter Twelve

Who would have guessed there could be so many vintage clothes in Mudville? so many vintage clothes in Mudville?

It was nine o'clock, and the place was hopping. I had been busy in the kitchen with Aunt Stella until now, but the food orders were mostly done now. Karaoke was about to start.

I made my way over to the table where Brent and Tara were sitting.

Brent gave me a big smile. He patted the chair next to him, and I sat.

"You heard?" I said. "About Harry not being Earl?"

Brent nodded. He had slicked back his hair and was dressed like a fifties bad boy.

"Guess we didn't tell you," Tara said, leaning over. "Most people like to dress the part when we have one of these nights."

"You look terrific!" I said. Tara had on a pink fluffy sweater and a round circle skirt. And I had to admit, Brent, in jeans and a white T-shirt with the sleeve rolled up on one side to hold a pack of cigarettes, looked hotter than ever.

"Where's Simon?" I asked.

"He'll be here soon," said Brent. "He likes to make an entrance."

"Just wait," said Tara. She and Brent exchanged grins.

Most of the Big Dill customers were doing their best to channel the early days of rock and roll. But not Vern. He was wearing his usual getup. He came over and joined our table. Aunt Stella followed him and sat down.

"Looks like a casting call for *Happy Days*," Vern said.

"You're just an old grump," said my aunt. "Everyone else is dressed the part."

"Now Stella," said Vern, "you know I don't go in for this primping crap." He looked embarrassed.

"Where are Jean and Dotty Dot?" Aunt Stella glanced toward the back door. "They always go in for fifties night in a big way."

"You're right. Isn't like them to be late," said Vern.

"Here we go," said my aunt. Karaoke was about to start.

"Oh no," said Vern, looking at the makeshift stage. "It's Larry. I need cheese."

"Cheese?" I said.

"Makes good earplugs."

A bald man in unfortunately tight jeans had taken the mic and was squeaking along to "Big Girls Don't Cry." I was a big girl, and I wanted to cry. *Maybe I should take out the garbage.* I quietly rose from the table and tiptoed to the kitchen.

It was a clear night, a glorious night. The quarter moon looked like it had been painted onto a coal-black satin sky. I plunked the bag down into the garbage can and secured the top. Then I stepped back to breathe in the fresh air.

Already I was feeling at home here. I had made friends. I'd met a guy who made my blood race. I missed Mom, but she would be here soon. It was totally unexpected, this good feeling I had about Mudville.

The song ended, thankfully. I could hear polite applause. It was safe to return. I grabbed the handle of the old wooden door and pulled it open.

That's when something amazing happened. A voice came over the sound system. A one-in-a-million voice. Was Elvis alive? Or had his ghost dropped into the Dilly tonight?

I stepped out from the kitchen to see who was crooning "Can't Help Falling in Love."

It was Simon.

Hair slicked back, eyes closed, both hands hugging the mic, Simon swayed back and forth on the stage. His golden voice filled the room. Everyone was spellbound.

At the end of the song, applause exploded. Someone yelled, "Do 'Hound Dog'!"

Simon smiled like an angel. And then he started to sing again. One arm shot to the air. I watched, astonished, as his normally gawky body transformed into that of a one sexy dance king. Who knew?

I sat down beside Brent. "Fantastic, isn't he?" said Brent.

I nodded.

"I can't believe Dotty is missing this!" Aunt Stella whispered. "Hope nothing's wrong."

Applause shook the room when Simon finished his encore. People were on their feet, hollering for more.

I was closest to the back door and saw it edge open.

Jean stumbled in. She was dressed like Tara was, in a full skirt and fluffy sweater. But the look on her face made the costume seem like a horrid joke.

Her eyes found Aunt Stella and focused. Her mouth opened. For a moment I thought she was going to collapse.

The room fell silent.

"What is it?" asked my aunt, rising from the chair.

"It's Dotty," said Jean, her voice a frog's croak. "She fell down the basement stairs. I think she's dead."

Chapter Thirteen

I learned something that night. In small communities, people come together. They cry together. They mourn together. They hold you when you need to be held.

I became a part of the community that night. It felt good, in a sad, sad way.

When I finally got back to my room, I wrote an email to Dad. I told him everything. About finding the bones. About investigating with my friends. About the police eliminating Earl based on his DNA. About Dotty falling down the stairs. Before I saved it to Drafts, I signed off by saying I loved him.

You never know when you're going to lose someone.

Dad must have written back immediately. I picked it up the next morning.

This is serious, Penny. I don't think you realize the danger. A body has been discovered. The killer is still at large. After all these years, he thinks he's safe. And now there has been another death. Think about it. Trust me. I know about these things. Don't get involved. You hear me? Take protection wherever you go.

I was a little shook up. What was he talking about? Another death? He must mean Dotty. But that was just an accident. Wasn't it?

I thought about my dad's words while getting ready to meet Tara. And about what he had said about taking protection. Ollie couldn't come with me today. Instead, I would take Ollie's bag.

It was nearly ten when Tara pulled into the parking lot. Tara had borrowed Brent's car for the shopping trip. We were going to buy clothes for Dotty's funeral. I had nothing suitable. And I wanted to show respect. If there is one thing a mob connection teaches you, it's the importance of showing respect.

"I left Wolfgang at home," she said as I stepped out of the pub. "He's not impressed."

"Tara, what are you *wearing*?"

She looked down at the ratty brown cardigan she had on. "What? I got chilly.

It was in the backseat. I think it's Brent's."

I shook my head. "Brent would never wear anything that nasty."

"Then it's probably Dad's," she said, not seeming to care.

I rolled my eyes. Wearing that old thing? How could she not care? It had holes in it! So not cool. I was going to have to lend her something of mine. A sweatshirt maybe. Or a jacket.

A jacket. Wait a minute...

My mouth went dry. My forehead felt prickly.

"Holy crap, Tara." I paused, as the jigsaw puzzles came into place in my mind. "I just thought of something important."

Tara waited without speaking. She could probably tell that my mind was working triple-time. Yes. It could be. I needed to talk to—

"Simon's uncle, the cop. Bob? I need to talk to him. Can you text Simon?"

Tara handed me her phone. "You can do it."

I quickly fired off a text.

It's Penny. Ask Bob asap. Did he ever take Jean's DNA?

Simon replied immediately. **Will do. Why?**

I didn't wait to respond.

"Tara, we've got to get to Jean's house." I grabbed her arm and started pulling her toward the sidewalk. It would be faster to go on foot.

"Okay, but will you tell me what's going on?" she said.

"We learned it in school last year. Family members have a lot of the same DNA. It can show if people are related."

"Yeah. So?"

I felt out of breath, but I got it out. "The DNA on the jacket Jean gave the police didn't match the DNA of the corpse. So we all ruled out Earl as the victim."

She was running to keep up with me now.

"Remember what Aunt Stella said? *Nobody ever throws out things in this town.*"

"I'm still not quite following you. Why did you ask about Jean's DNA?"

I was at Jean's door now. I rang the doorbell. I couldn't hear anything inside. I tried the door. It opened.

"Nobody ever locks doors in this town either," muttered Tara.

My right hand reached into Ollie's bag for the handgun. I heard Tara gasp. I walked into the house. It was dead quiet inside. "Jean?" I called out. No answer.

"Penny, is this smart?" asked Tara nervously. "Shouldn't we leave this to the cops?"

I looked around for something of Jean's to swipe for a DNA test. Nothing was in the front hall. I peered into the front room where we had sat having tea. No one was there.

I carried on to the kitchen at the back, hoping to find a used teacup or spoon. The kitchen was old and worn, but clean. *Very* clean—almost eerie. Nothing on the counters. Everything put away in cupboards. Like Jean had gone away.

A single envelope was propped up on the old wooden table.

Please give to the authorities, said the note written on it.

My heart was in my throat. I put the gun down on the table and snatched up the envelope. I ripped it open.

I only had to read a few lines. "Oh man. I was right," I said to Tara. "Listen to this."

I read the letter out loud.

"I expect you've guessed by now. Or maybe not.

"I want to say that none of this was intended. It wasn't planned or anything. I'm very, very sorry for everything. If I have any defense, it would be that things were so different back then. There were some things you just couldn't be honest about.

"Sally and Earl weren't having an affair.

"Here's what really happened:

"Earl was away on one of his many fishing trips. I thought the coast was clear. So I made plans to stay overnight with Sally at the Dilly. It wasn't the first time.

"It was simply bad luck that Earl came back early. When I didn't come home that night, he went searching for me. He came to the pub. Earl saw me coming out of Sally's bedroom to go to the washroom. I wasn't wearing any clothes.

"Earl went berserk. He called me all sorts of horrible names and started hitting me. He knocked me to the floor. That's when Sally came up behind him and hit him with a baseball bat. I'm pretty sure he would have killed me if she hadn't.

"Sally was marvelous. Like one of the furies. He was so heavy, there was no way we could get him to the lake. She suggested we bury him right in the backyard."

I stopped reading for a minute to catch my breath. "Call the police," I said to Tara. She nodded and pulled out her cell phone.

I continued reading to myself.

We stripped Earl and put all his belongings into a duffel bag. Sally left town with the bag. I was the one who spread the rumor that Sally and Earl had run off together.

It looked like everything would be fine. And for years it was. Then that dog dug up the body.

I honestly don't know what happened to me then. When Dotty started to prattle on, I panicked.

Dotty. Dear Dotty Dot. She was so dear to me. But I couldn't trust her anymore. She'd suddenly remember something and blurt it right out. When she starting asking people if it was Earl, I nearly died.

You've got to believe I didn't plan it. It must have been a kind of insanity. I can't believe I pushed her down the stairs. A split-second decision that I regretted instantly.

I'm going to the cabin. Stella knows where it is. But by the time you find this, the pills will have done their job. Please tell everyone how sorry I am.

Jean

Chapter Fourteen

Hours later, we were all hanging out at the Dilly.

"And you figured this out how?" asked Brent. I liked how he looked at me. It felt good to be admired.

"She was amazing," said Tara. I gave her a quick smile.

"Tara gave me the clue," I said. "It was the ratty old sweater she was wearing."

"Still is, actually," said Simon, poking her in the arm. I glanced at the two of them. Definitely something going on between them.

"Tara said it was her dad's sweater. Then I remembered what Aunt Stella had said. That people never throw things out in this town. For some reason I thought of Jean. She had given the police a jacket so they could check for Earl's DNA. An old hunting jacket. But what if it wasn't Earl's jacket? What if it was her dad's?"

"So…the DNA on it wouldn't match the bones," said Brent, catching on quickly.

"That is really clever," said Simon. I didn't know if he meant me or Jean.

"So then I thought, why would Jean deliberately mislead the police?"

"So you figured out she was having an affair with Sally Hooke?" Brent asked.

"Not at first. I was going on the assumption that Earl was, like everyone else thought. And that that's why Jean killed him," I paused. "And then I remembered what Sally Hooke's niece said."

They all looked at me. "Don't you remember, Tara? She said she couldn't imagine Aunt Sally running off with this guy," I said. "That she had never cared much about men."

"Oh, right," said Tara, groaning. "That slipped right by me."

"I know she was a murderer, but I do feel sorry for Jean. It must have been awful to hide who she truly was," said Simon. He was right. I had been so excited about solving the mystery. But now I could imagine the pain Jean must have endured. I knew a thing or two about secrets and how heavy a burden they can be.

None of us spoke for a while.

Finally Brent broke the silence. "So you were going to confront Jean? That's pretty brave."

"No," I said. "I just wanted to get something of Jean's so they could compare her DNA to what they got from the jacket. My makeshift plan was to make up an excuse for the visit and then pocket something when she wasn't looking. Gloves, a scarf—anything with her DNA on it. If Jean gave them her dad's jacket instead of Earl's, the police would have been able to tell."

"Wow," said Brent again. "You're really good at this."

"Everyone helped," I said. "If Tara hadn't worn that jacket…if you hadn't been able to trace Sally Hooke…"

"Even the dogs," said Simon. "If Ollie and Wolfgang hadn't dug up that bone…"

I looked over at the two dogs, snuggled up together on the floor. So nice that Ollie had found a friend.

"I know!" said Tara, beaming. "The four of us should form a club. The Crime Club. We could meet regularly to learn about how to be PIs. And then we could investigate mysteries together."

I liked the sound of that. A Crime Club with the four of us. It would mean we would have a reason to get together a lot. I looked over at Brent. He was smiling at me.

"Great idea!" said Simon. "Maybe we could even make some money at it."

Tara glared at him. "We're not doing this to make money. We have a higher calling. Making sure the wrong people don't get blamed for stuff."

I laid my hand palm down on the table. "Let's make this happen," I said.

Brent put his right hand on mine. Tara put hers on top of his. Simon put his on hers.

"To the Crime Club!" said Brent. "And to new friends." He winked at me.

I smiled back. It was a good start. We'd get better at investigating. And then maybe one day I'd find out what really happened with my dad.

Acknowledgments

Two years ago I was signing books at an Orca booth. Two teachers came up to me and told me that my mysteries featuring the crime-solving goddaughter of a notorious mob boss were very popular in their high school. So why wasn't I writing YA?

I want to thank those teachers today. I've come back to my roots with *Crime Club*. I was that kid with my nose in a mystery book all the time. It was my fervent dream to someday write for teens. It only took me fifteen books to get to it.

Many thanks to the people in my life who provide encouragement and support.

Front of the pack are my husband, Dave, and daughters, Natalie and Alex. I also depend on Cathy Astolfo, Janet Bolin, Alison Bruce, Cheryl Freedman, Don and Ruth Graves, Jeannette Harrison, Joan O'Callaghan and Nancy O'Neil. Thank you, dear friends.

Crime Club was a labor of love from start to finish. Tanya Trafford and the wonderful team at Orca books have made it better.

Melodie Campbell is the award-winning author of several works of fiction, including the Gina Gallo Mystery series in the Rapid Reads collection. Melodie lives in Oakville, Ontario.

9781459822351 PB

"Another package for you," I said, tossing it onto Tom's lap.

"Oh, good. Probably the audio interface." Tom started ripping into the box. "What took you so long?"

"Gary. The guy makes what should be a ten-second delivery into an awkward, ten-minute chat."

Tom grinned. "Is he your new friend, Charlie?" Gary is a legend in our house.

Uncle Dave and Mom hide, literally *hide*, when they see him stumbling up the walk.

"Yeah, right. The guy is *nosy*. Isn't it illegal or something for a mail carrier to ask what's in your mail?" Then, not caring that I was being nosy too, I asked, "How much are you spending on all this stuff?"

"None of your business. Not *tons*. Some of my job money."

Tom works at Sport Shed. *Worked* at Sport Shed. Maybe he will again when he can actually walk around.

"Oh, hey. There's been another couple of break-and-enters in the neighborhood. That's what Gary said. I don't know if we can believe him."

"Really? Jeez. Mom will freak."

"Gary could be making things up for a little drama. A bit of excitement. He's in full crime-fighter mode."

"That's *all* we need," said Tom, laughing.

"Look, you want anything else? Got your medicine? Water? I'm going to go for a walk."

"Nope, I'm good," Tom said. He was studying the instruction manual for the electronic blah-blah he'd just gotten. I grabbed the cereal bowls. One empty, one a soggy mess. Tom looked up. "Thanks, buddy."

"No prob." Tom was, in fact, a really good guy. My best friend, if I wanted to get all emotional about it. So mostly I didn't mind doing stuff for him. I knew he'd do the same for me.

I ran down to the kitchen to unload. I noticed a blinking light on the answering machine.

Hi, this is Carly Silberman from the office at Walter Watts High School. I'm calling about Charlie's absence from school. We'll just need a note to confirm—

I pushed *Delete*. I had told Mom the school was okay with my taking a week off to help Tom.

"That's so good of them!" she had said. "They must know how close you guys are. And you're such a good student, Charlie. Missing a few days shouldn't affect your grades at all."

What I didn't tell Mom was that I had lied. I had been emailing notes about my absences all week as Mom— Gloria Swift.

I wanted to help Mom out. She had been working double shifts lately. She was worried about how Tom was going to manage on his own. Uncle Dave was out all the time "job hunting." There was only me.

Thing is, I desperately needed a break from my new school anyway. I was doing great, grades-wise. I had a much higher average than Tom. But high school isn't only about grades. It's not even mostly about grades. I needed a break from walking the halls alone. From timing my arrival to make sure I got to school right at the bell so I didn't have to stand alone in the hall. From pretending to talk on my cell phone at lunch so nobody thought I was a loser.

Other than us both having dark hair and blue eyes, Tom and I looked very different, that was a fact. He was tall, I was short (but really hoping for a growth spurt). He was athletic, I was not. He was relaxed and easygoing and popular. I was none of those things.

Mom had no idea how miserable my life was. Even if she did, she would say I needed to give it time. To make friends at a new school, to feel more comfortable there. I knew all that. But it didn't make it any easier. And I wasn't about to start worrying her with my problems.

Tom's injury had been the perfect opportunity for me to take a break.

As I stacked the bowls in the dishwasher and wiped down the kitchen counter, I planned my route. I was going to walk past the two houses that just got broken into and see if I could gather any information. Clues. Observations.

Maybe the police needed a bit of help solving these break-ins. An extra pair of eyes. Somebody who knew the neighborhood. Somebody who would blend right in.

Somebody who had no idea what he was getting himself into.